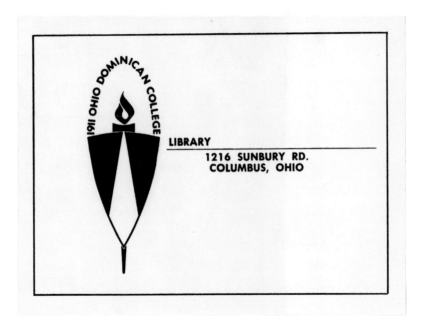

When the Sky Is Like Lace

by Elinor Lander Horwitz

Pictures by Barbara Cooney

J. B. Lippincott Company/Philadelphia and New York

For my nieces:

Angela
Reyna
and
Eve

J
H

U.S. Library of Congress Cataloging in Publication Data

Horwitz, Elinor Lander.   When the sky is like lace.

SUMMARY: Describes the strange and splendid things that can happen on a bimulous night when the sky is like lace.   [1. Fantasy] I. Cooney, Barbara, birth date   II. Title.

PZ7.H7925WL   [E]   75-9664   ISBN-0-397-31550-3

On a bimulous night, the sky is like lace.

Do you know how it looks when it's bimulous and
the sky is like lace?

It doesn't happen often, but when it does—

KA-BOOM!

—and everything is strange-splendid and plum-purple.

One thing that happens on bimulous nights when the sky is like lace is that the otters sing. They sing and sing all night long whether anyone asks them to or not.

The otters only know one song, which is rather nasty. They sing it to the tune of the "Mexican Hat Dance," but you can sing it to any tune you like. It goes like this:

> Oh, all snails look just like each other;
> Can you tell any one from another?
> Little brother is just like his sister.
> Who could ever tell missus from mister?

This insults the snails, of course. Each snail believes that he is quite different from all other snails, very much himself. So when the otters sing their nasty song on bimulous nights, the snails usually sulk under the cinnamon bush until the moon is high. Then they line up two by two and march down to the grove to watch the trees dance.

Because on bimulous nights when the sky is like lace, the trees eucalyptus back and forth, forth and back, swishing and swaying, swaying and swishing—in the fern-deep grove at the midnight end of the garden.

You will also find that, on bimulous nights when the sky is like lace, the grass is like gooseberry jam. It's not really squooshy like jam, because then the otters' feet would slurp around and the snails might drown. It only *smells* like gooseberry jam. But if you walk barefoot, it feels like the velvet inside a very old violin case.

If you plan to go out on a bimulous night when the sky is like lace, here are some rules you must remember:

Never talk to a rabbit or a kissing gourami.
If your nose itches, don't scratch it.
Wear nothing that is orange, not even underneath.

And—if you have a lucky penny, put it in your pocket. Because, on bimulous nights when the sky is like lace and the otters are singing and the snails are sulking and the trees are dancing and the grass is like gooseberry jam, it's a good idea to be prepared.

Because—you never know.

The next thing to talk about is the eating. On nights when it's bimulous and the sky is like lace, the thing to eat is spaghetti with pineapple sauce. It's hard to say why this is so, and yet it's always been done.

You might even say it's a custom.

After the eating comes the singing. Here's a new
song you might like to teach the otters. It's called
"The Katydid" and you'll have to make up the tune
yourself because it doesn't have one.

> Katy didn't do it.
> No, Katy didn't do it.
> Ask the goose and ask the gander;
> Who thought up this bit of slander?
> When the owls were told, they booed it.
> When the cows got wind, they mooed it.
> When the pigeons heard, they cooed it.
> Katy didn't
> Katy didn't
> Katy didn't do it.

After the singing come the presents. On bimulous nights when the sky is like lace, everyone exchanges presents like

three fireflies in a jar
anything chartreuse
honey
kites
home-made marshmallow fudge
a bag of red marbles
a coconut

After the eating, the singing, and the presents, on
nights when it's bimulous and the sky is like lace, and
after the trees have stopped dancing, you might want to

  ride a camel bareback
  juggle three peaches
  gather cornflowers
  dig clams
  shout and yell and hop up and down in the mud
  pretend to be a helicopter
  play dominoes
  tickle an elephant

Pick any two you like best.

The last bimulous night happened three weeks ago
Wednesday before Tuesday.

Did you hear the otters sing?
    The wind was rather whistly that night.
Did you see the trees dance the eucalyptus?
    There were plum-purple shadows on the bedroom
    ceiling.
Did you see that the sky was like lace?
    Or did you fall asleep and miss it?

You had better be prepared next time.

Here's what you should do. Each night from now on look out the window at the man in the moon through a clean white handkerchief before you get into bed. If he winks his left eye, that's the signal. Start cooking spaghetti and plan to be up all night.

And please take care not to speak to a rabbit or a kissing gourami.

And if your nose itches, don't scratch it.

And be sure not to put on anything orange—not even underneath.

Because you don't want to miss a thing

when

    the otters are tuning their voices

    and the snails are lining up two by two

    and the trees are aslant at the midnight end of the
        garden

    and the sky—the sky—OH, LOOK AT THE SKY!

It's going to be
PERFECTLY BIMULOUS!

98471

DATE DUE

JY 21 '76	NOV 21 1983	
OC 26 '76	DEC 1 1989	
MAR 31 '77	OCT 15 1991	
APR 3 '78	SEP. 12 1993	
FEB 20 '80		
MAR 0 1 '80		
MAR 12 '80		
DEC 22 '81		
FEB 27 '82		
FEB 0 0 1982 FACULTY		
OCT 10 1983		